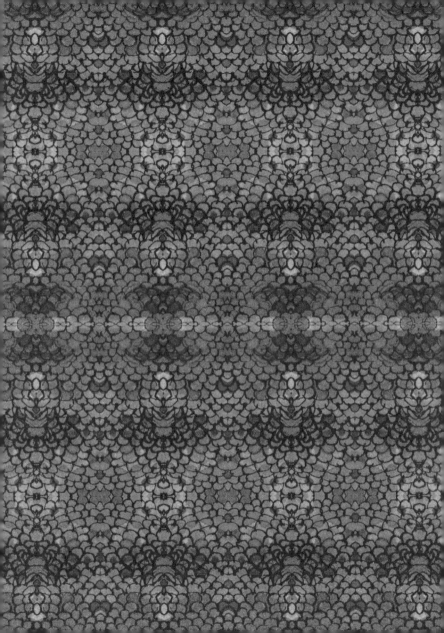

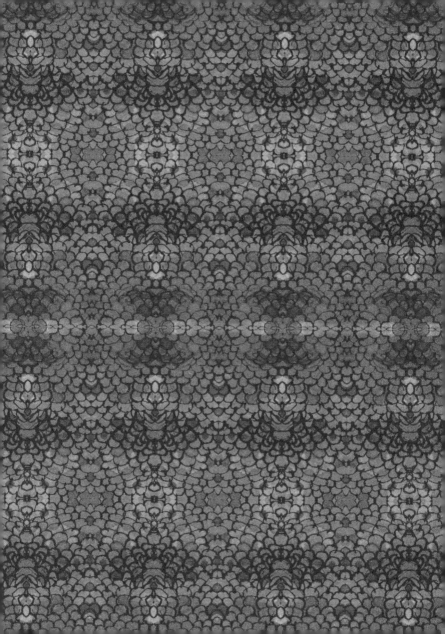

MONSTER BUSTERS

MONSTER BUSTERS

Cornelia Funke

With illustrations by
Glenys Ambrus

Barrington Stoke

First published in Great Britain in 2015 by
Barrington Stoke Ltd
18 Walker Street, Edinburgh, EH3 7LP

www.barringtonstoke.co.uk

Title of the original German edition:
Leselöwen – Monstergeschichten
© 1993 Loewe Verlag GmbH, Bindlach

Illustrations © 2015 Glenys Ambrus
Translation © 2015 Barrington Stoke

The moral right of Cornelia Funke and Glenys Ambrus to
be identified as the author and illustrator of this work has
been asserted in accordance with the Copyright, Designs and
Patents Act, 1988

A CIP catalogue record for this book is available from the
British Library upon request

ISBN: 978-1-78112-396-6

Printed in China by Leo

This book has dyslexia friendly features

Contents

Chapter 1
Cowardy Custard

It was the holidays. And the best thing about the holidays was the fun fair.

Rosa loved fun fairs. She loved candy floss, roller coasters and Ferris wheels. But, most of all, Rosa loved ghost trains.

Rosa loved the ghosts, the monsters and the rattly skeletons. She loved the scuttly spiders and the creepy crawlies.

The fun fair came to town just after school closed for the holidays. Rosa went along with her best friend, Ivan. They ate some candy floss and went on all the new rides. Last of all, they went to the ghost train.

Rosa jumped up and down with joy. "Wow!" she said. "Look how scary it is this year."

"I've got goose bumps already," Ivan said. "I don't like the look of that big monster mouth at all. It's too scary."

"Cowardy custard," Rosa said. "If you're too yellow, I'll go by myself. I'm not scared – I'm a monster buster!"

The same thing happened every year. Ivan wouldn't go anywhere near the ghost train. So Rosa left him standing there. She got her ticket and climbed into the train. The big monster mouth swallowed her up and she vanished into the darkness.

All around her, Rosa could hear groans and moans and sighs. A skeleton grabbed her hair. A massive spider's web swung into her face.

Rosa's skin went all goose-bumpy.

"Ooh, it's even more horrible this year!" she said. "I hope they still have the big snake, and the vampire and – Oh!"

Rosa stared in surprise. There was something new. It was a disgusting monster with the longest arms Rosa had ever seen. It leaned out of the darkness

so that its huge claws dangled over the tracks of the train.

"Googly moogly!" Rosa shook with disgust. The monster's claws were so scary. And it looked so real!

The train took Rosa closer and closer to the bendy legs of the monster.

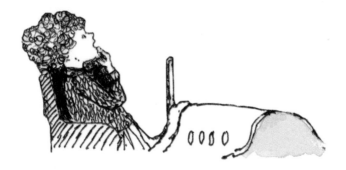

Then a shout came from above.
"Waa ha ha haaa!"

Rosa looked up and saw the
monster's mouth. It was twisted into an
evil grin.

Rosa crouched back down in fear.
But then a massive claw shot down and
scooped her out of her seat and up into
the dark!

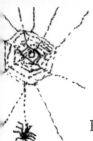

Help!" Rosa shouted. "H-help!"

"Ha ha ha ha ha!" the monster laughed. It dangled poor Rosa right in front of its nasty glittery eyes.

"Let me down!" Rosa sobbed. "You are horrid. What do you want from me?"

"I want some company!" the monster growled. It blew its stinky breath into

Rosa's face. "I'm bored to death of all the pretend ghosts and skeletons in here!"

"So – so the others aren't real then?" Rosa stammered.

"Real?" the monster said. "Silly girl! Of course they're not real. They're made from cardboard. Bah!"

The monster showed its terrible teeth and swung its claw over one of the trains as it rattled past. "It's dead boring, having to frighten humans all the time!" it moaned.

Rosa closed her eyes. She didn't dare look down, but she didn't dare look at the monster either.

"Come on, open your eyes and tell me a story!" the monster snarled at her.

"I don't know any stories," Rosa said in a small voice. "Please let me down now!"

"If you don't know a story," the monster grunted, "I will just have to eat you!" And he sniffed at Rosa from head to toe.

"No!" Rosa shouted. She kicked her legs as hard as she could. "Ivan!" she screamed. "Help!"

"Rosa!" a voice shouted from below. "Rosa, where are you?"

"Up here!" Rosa shouted so hard that her head almost exploded. "The new monster has –"

A smelly claw pressed down on her mouth. "Shut up or I will eat you NOW!" the monster growled. "Who is this Ivan?"

"A monster buster," Rosa whispered. "He is a very famous monster buster."

"Well," the monster said with an evil grin. "If that's true, I'd better eat you now!" It smacked its lips and opened its mouth – and then it let out an ear-splitting howl of pain.

"Oooooow!"

The monster's claws let go of Rosa and she fell down like a stone.

"Aaa!" Rosa cried as she landed head first on a strange rubber-blubber creature on the floor of the ghost train.

"Come on, Rosa!" she heard Ivan say.

Ivan dragged Rosa back into the train. Above their heads, they could hear the monster's angry shouts.

The train shot past two skeletons, three ghosts and one dragon – and then Rosa and Ivan were back outside.

Rosa blinked in the bright sun as she looked at her friend. "How on earth did you do that?" she asked.

Ivan grinned from ear to ear. "I bit it," he said. "I bit that horrid monster's little toe. It tasted awful!"

Rosa grinned back at him. "Thank you," she said. "I'm glad it turned out that you're the real monster buster after all!"

Chapter 2
Safe at School

After Rosa's scare on the ghost train, she was very glad to get back to school.

The first day back was a horrid rainy day. The children were soaking wet and grumpy.

Drops of rain fell from their hair onto the pages of their jotters and little puddles formed around their shoes.

At 9 o'clock on the dot, the classroom door opened and in came the plump Head Teacher. She was followed by a thin little man with a red face, a friendly smile and a diamond pattern on his jumper.

"Good morning, children!" the Head
Teacher said. "This is Mr Troll, your new
teacher."

"Mr Troll?" Rosa said. "Oh, no!"

Everyone giggled. The Head Teacher left the room and Mr Troll sat down behind a desk that was far too big for him.

"Typical!" he said. "Why does it have to rain today of all days?" He sighed and felt his pointed nose. He had a worried look on his face.

"What's so bad about rain?" Fred asked from the red group's table. "It's always raining here."

"Is it?" Mr Troll's eyes opened wide with horror. "Oh no, that's no good at all!"

As Mr Troll spoke, his nose began to spread and stretch. The children watched as it grew longer and longer and wider and wider.

Then it grew bristles like an old
broom. Mr Troll's ears grew big and
pointy like two white traffic cones. And
then the new teacher started to change
colour all over. He turned a nasty shade
of poison green – only the diamond
pattern on his jumper stayed the same.

"Oh no! I just knew this would happen!" Mr Troll cried. "But why did it have to happen today? I am so sorry. Watch out, everyone!"

Mr Troll raised his poison-green finger to warn the children. And then he started to grow. And grow. And grow!

Rosa, Ivan, Izzy and Boris hid with Fred under the red group's table. They watched from this shelter as their new teacher grew bigger and bigger until he filled half the classroom like a huge green balloon.

With a sudden stretch, Mr Troll ripped the coat pegs off the wall. Great spikes had grown on his head, like a dinosaur, and the spikes knocked a huge hole in the ceiling. Then his long and jagged tail smashed the whiteboard and he used the huge sharp claws on his left arm to push on the door.

"Nooooo!" the entire class moaned.

"Wow!" Fred said. "Wowee!"

And then the big green monster
at the teacher's desk smiled at the
children. It was a friendly smile – even
with its long, sharp teeth.

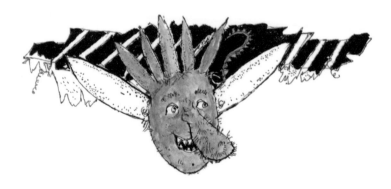

Then it spoke in Mr Troll's kind voice. "Not to worry, children," it said. "This only happens when it rains."

And then Mr Troll puffed out a bright yellow flame. The flame dried everyone's wet hair in an instant and made all the children giggle.

"What on earth is all this noise?" the Head Teacher roared from outside the classroom door. But Mr Troll's sharp claws were still holding the door shut. And so, no matter how hard the Head Teacher rattled the door, she could not get in.

All of a sudden, a ray of sunshine came through the window and fell on Mr Troll's green nose.

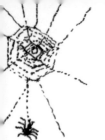

Pfffft!

It was as if someone had let the air out of a big balloon.

Pfft!

The huge green monster turned back into the shy, skinny new teacher.

The Head Teacher fell in the open
door of the classroom.

"What's going on here?" she yelled
in horror. She pointed at the smashed
whiteboard, the upside-down desk, and
the holes in the wall where the pegs had
been.

"Oh, I'm so sorry. That was me," Mr Troll said with an embarrassed smile. "I seem to have been a little clumsy."

The Head Teacher's mouth fell open. But no words came out.

The class couldn't stop laughing.

Ivan and Rosa looked at the Head
Teacher and at Mr Troll, their strange
new teacher.

"You know what, Ivan?" Rosa said.
"I hope it rains a lot this year!"

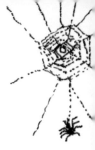

Chapter 3
Monster Munch

Far, far away in the mountains above
the town where Rosa and Ivan lived,
there was a big, grumpy and altogether
horrid monster called Grubbybats. He
lived high up in the mountains, where
there is nothing but ice, snow and
stones.

For more than 3,000 years, Grubbybats had lived in a pitch-black cave all by himself. His tummy had rumbled for most of that time.

Day in, day out, Grubbybats had only stones to eat. There was nothing else to be had – just an unlucky hiker or a squirrel now and then.

But the stones gave Grubbybats the most terrible tummy ache. And, after all those years, Grubbybats was really sick of tummy ache, and really really sick of stones.

So every day, from sunrise until late into the night, Grubbybats would lie in wait. He waited and waited and hoped and hoped that a careless, tasty creature would get lost and wander past his cave.

And one day – at long last – a school bus packed full of children lost its way. It ended up high in the mountains, in the place of ice and snow and stones where Grubbybats lived.

Grubbybats spotted the bus from far away as it crawled its way up the narrow mountain road. He licked his lips and grinned. It was a hungry and not-very-nice grin.

The bus looked like a tasty and filling snack.

All Grubbybats had to do was to push a big rock into the middle of the narrow mountain path. The rest was as easy as anything.

Of course, the children on the bus did not realise that they were now on the menu of a terrible and very hungry monster.

The children were too busy singing songs.

"Stop the bus, I need a wee wee,

Stop the bus I need a wee wee,

Stop the bus I need a wee wee ..."

The children were still singing when the bus screeched to a stop.

The bus driver stared at the massive rock that was blocking the road ahead. She was very puzzled.

"Well, I never!" she said to herself as she scratched her head. "Watch out, everyone! We have to turn around!"

Everyone's hair stood on end as the driver turned the bus on the narrow road. Then she drove straight into a tunnel.

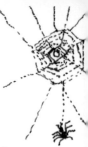

"How strange!" the bus driver said, as the world turned pitch black. "That tunnel wasn't here a moment ago."

But it was too late.

Grubbybats the monster was horrible and hungry – but he was not at all stupid.

He had lain down on the road,
opened his stinky mouth and rolled out
his huge green tongue.

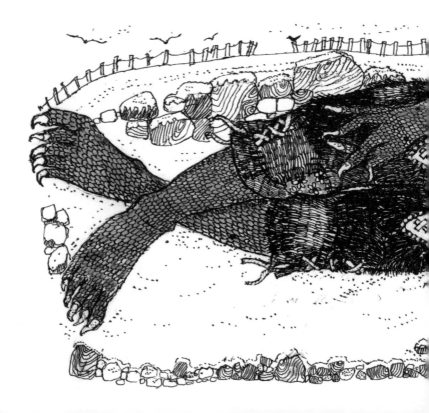

And the bus, with its tasty load of school children, had driven straight into his empty tummy.

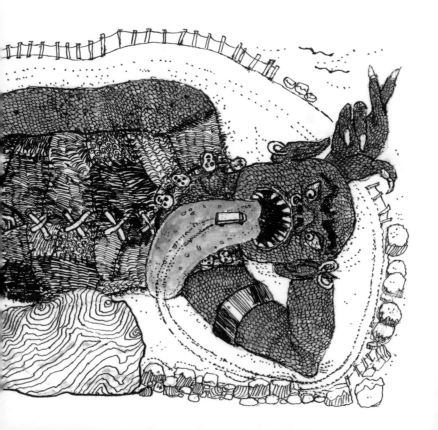

"Guuulp!" went the terrible Grubbybats. "GUUULLP!"

He burped.

"BUUURP!"

Then he licked his nasty lips and dragged himself back to his cave for a little after-dinner nap.

Chapter 4
To the Rescue

"Where on earth are we?" Mr Troll
cried. He looked back at his class – his
swallowed class of school children,
who were now deep, deep down in
Grubbybats's tummy.

"It looks like a cave of some sort to
me!" the bus driver muttered. She didn't

look too worried. She was too busy tucking into her packed lunch.

"In any case, we can't go any further," she told Mr Troll.

"We're not in a cave! We're in a stomach," Rosa said. She had a book called 'The Body' and she was very interested in the subject. "Did you not see the jagged teeth when we drove in, Mr Troll?"

"That's right," Ivan said. "It was a mouth. A massive mouth. Like a ghost train. I think it was a monster."

The other children nodded. Ivan was right – he was always right.

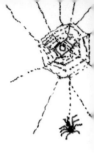

Mr Troll and the bus driver looked at each other in astonishment. Then they rushed over to the windows and looked out.

"Oh my word," Mr Troll cried in horror. "Look at all those skeletons everywhere."

"Hmm!" the driver said. She scratched her head to help her think. "It looks like we have been eaten by something."

"Why don't we start the engine again?" Ivan said out loud. "The fumes will make the monster feel sick and he will spit us out again."

"Yes, and what about the radio?"
Rosa said. "Let's turn the radio on full
blast. The noise will upset the monster's
tummy!"

The bus driver sat down behind the
wheel again and smiled.

"All right then, I will drive round and round!" she said. "Let's see how the monster likes that."

"And will you lot start singing your awful song again?" Mr Troll asked. "That really does sound terrible."

Grubbybats was snoring peacefully in his cave when something very odd happened in his tummy.

Terrible, smelly clouds of smoke started to come out of his ears and nose.

Huge bumps appeared on his tummy and it hurt like mad.

Awful noises came from his insides. He had never heard such awful noises before.

"What the blazes!" Grubbybats cried. "What on earth is going on in my normally peaceful insides?"

Grubbybats could not stop burping and his face turned scarlet.

He rolled around in the snow in front of his cave in a terrible panic.

Most times the cold snow helped when he had tummy ache, but this time it only made it worse.

At long last, a massive cough made Grubbybats spit his tasty meal out again. It flew right out of his mouth in a huge, high arc.

The battered bus landed with a bump on its wheels. The driver sped away as fast as she could, with a terrified glance in her rear-view mirror. And, with that, the tasty snack that had been so hard to digest swerved off with a screech and a squeal.

"Googly moogly! Would you look at that!" Mr Troll cried. He stared out of the rear window with a look of horror on his face.

There, behind them, stood the horrible and hungry Grubbybats.

He towered over the road like a skyscraper. And he was sticking his huge green tongue out at the school bus as it sped off back down the mountain pass.

"Wow," Ivan said to Rosa. "That was a close shave, even for a pair of monster busters."

The bus sped off down the mountain and Grubbybats stood and watched until it was gone.

"What a racket," he groaned. He could still hear the terrible noise of a bus full of children singing their awful song.

"Stop the bus I need a wee wee,

Stop the bus I need a wee wee,

Stop the bus I need a wee wee,

And Mr Troll can't swim!"

Our books are tested
for children and young people by
children and young people.

Thanks to everyone who consulted on
a manuscript for their time and effort in
helping us to make our books better
for our readers.

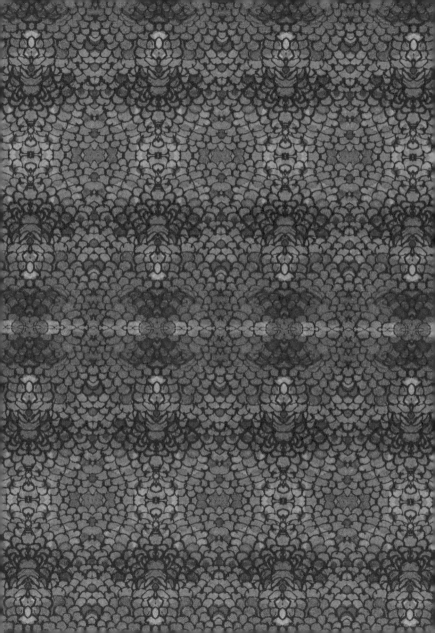

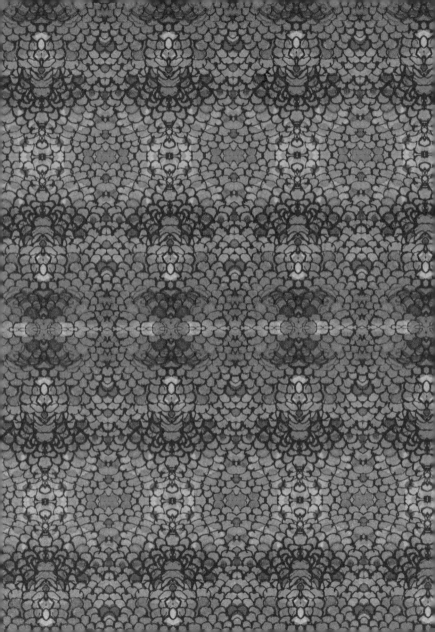